A Great Wilderness

Samuel D. Hunter

A SAMUEL FRENCH ACTING EDITION

SAMUEL
FRENCH

FOUNDED 1830

SAMUELFRENCH.COM
SAMUELFRENCH-LONDON.CO.UK

FOR PRODUCTION ENQUIRIES

UNITED STATES AND CANADA
Info@SamuelFrench.com
1-866-598-8449

UNITED KINGDOM AND EUROPE
Plays@SamuelFrench-London.co.uk
020-7255-4302

Each title is subject to availability from Samuel French, depending upon
country of performance. Please be aware that *A GREAT WILDERNESS*
may not be licensed by Samuel French in your territory. Professional
and amateur producers should contact the nearest Samuel French
office or licensing partner to verify availability.

MUSIC USE NOTE

Licensees are solely responsible for obtaining formal written permission from copyright owners to use copyrighted music in the performance of this play and are strongly cautioned to do so. If no such permission is obtained by the licensee, then the licensee must use only original music that the licensee owns and controls. Licensees are solely responsible and liable for all music clearances and shall indemnify the copyright owners of the play(s) and their licensing agent, Samuel French, against any costs, expenses, losses and liabilities arising from the use of music by licensees. Please contact the appropriate music licensing authority in your territory for the rights to any incidental music.

IMPORTANT BILLING AND CREDIT REQUIREMENTS

If you have obtained performance rights to this title, please refer to your licensing agreement for important billing and credit requirements.

A GREAT WILDERNESS was commissioned and first produced by Seattle Repertory Theater in January 2014. The performance was directed by Braden Abraham, with sets by Scott Bradley, costumes by Erik Andor, lights by LB Morse, sound by Obadiah Eaves, and dramaturgy by John M. Baker. The Production Stage Manager was Stina Lotti. The cast was as follows:

WALT	Michael Winters
ABBY	Christine Estabrook
DANIEL	Jack Taylor
EUNICE	Mari Nelson
JANET	Gretchen Krich
TIM	R. Hamilton Wright
VOICEOVER ON TV	Evan Whitfield

A GREAT WILDERNESS was then produced at the Williamstown Theatre Festival in July 2014. The performance was directed by Eric Ting, with sets by Wilson Chin, costumes by Jessica Pabst, lights by Matthew Richards, sound by Brandon Wolcott, and dramaturgy by John M. Baker. The Production Stage Manager was Lindsey Turteltaub. The cast was as follows:

WALT	Jeffrey DeMunn
ABBY	Mia Dillon
DANIEL	Stephan Amenta
EUNICE	Mia Barron
JANET	Tasha Lawrence
TIM	Kevin Geer
VOICEOVER ON TV	Claire Karwowski

A GREAT WILDERNESS was developed at The Eugene O'Neill Playwrights Conference (Preston Whiteway, Executive Director; Wendy Goldberg, Artistic Director) in 2013. It was directed by Braden Abraham.

CHARACTERS

WALT – Mid-seventies, male.

DANIEL – Sixteen, male.

ABBY – Mid-to-late sixties, female.

TIM – Mid-to-late sixties, male.

EUNICE – Forties or early fifties, female.

JANET – Late forties or early fifties, female.

VOICEOVER ON THE TELEVISION – Male or female.

SETTING

The common room of a decaying camp on the outskirts of a wilderness area in Idaho. There are full boxes everywhere, much of the space has been packed up. Only essential furniture remains, along with some camping gear, books including several numbered Bibles, a television, etc. A hallway leads to other bedrooms and a bathroom; a kitchen occupies a section of the stage.

AUTHOR'S NOTES

Dialogue written in italics is emphatic, deliberate; dialogue written in ALL CAPS is impulsive, explosive.

A "/" indicates an overlap in dialogue. Whenever a "/" appears, the following line of dialogue should begin.

The television frequently plays underneath the dialogue, and should be only slightly quieter than the actors. The effect should be that it's imposing, present – just short of irritating. The television dialogue is not always constant, but there should always be a twee, cheaply produced soundtrack playing in the background whenever the DVD is playing.

Dedicated to the memory of Jerry Manning.

ACT ONE

Scene One

(Late morning.)

*(***DANIEL*** *stands near the door holding a duffel bag. He looks around the room, obviously nervous.)*

*(***WALT*** *stands on the opposite end of the room, looking at him, smiling warmly.)*

(a tense silence)

WALT. Are you hungry? You've gotta be hungry.

(no response)

I think I have – there's plenty of food, you can help yourself to whatever you like. And I'll be cooking us our meals, I'm actually pretty good at, uh. Your mom probably told you all this, she –.

(no response)

Come in. Daniel. Please.

*(***DANIEL*** *pauses, then slowly moves inside, setting down his duffel.)*

WALT. Was your ride okay?

DANIEL. It was fine.

WALT. The ride up the mountain can be bumpy, a lot better than twenty years ago though, I'll tell you that much. And it's pretty, uh, was it pretty?

DANIEL. I don't –. I was sitting in the middle, / I didn't really –

WALT. Oh, that's –

DANIEL. I feel sort of turned around, I don't really feel like I know where I am right / now –

WALT. That's really a shame. Bobby should have let you sit up front, usually he lets my boys sit up front.

(pause)

DANIEL. The van was pretty full. Hunters or something.

WALT. Fishers, more likely. There's some very nice fly fishing around here. Bobby's been shuttling my boys up here for years / now –

DANIEL. "Your" boys? That's what you call us?

(pause)

WALT. Sorry, I –. I won't call you that if you don't –.

(short pause)

You're hungry. You've gotta be hungry.

(pause)

DANIEL. I'm okay.

*(**DANIEL** glances around the room a bit, his eyes land on the book on the podium.)*

WALT. Oh that's neat, take a look, you'll like it.

*(**WALT** goes to the book. **DANIEL** approaches it cautiously.)*

DANIEL. Is it a Bible?

WALT. No it's a dictionary, see –

*(**WALT** grabs the magnifying glass.)*

WALT. It's a compact edition of the complete Oxford English Dictionary, all twenty volumes in microprint. Here, look –

*(**WALT** motions for **DANIEL** to look through the magnifying glass.)*

Over five-hundred thousand words in here, you believe that?

DANIEL. Huh.

WALT. I've always loved dictionaries. Ugh, that makes me sound so boring, doesn't it? "I've always loved dictionaries."

DANIEL. Why?

WALT. I guess, I just – like knowing I have the help, if I need it. If I couldn't find the words.

(pause)

I'm not explaining myself very well. I just like dictionaries.

(awkward pause)

WALT. Are you sure you're not hungry?

(pause)

DANIEL. Okay.

WALT. Sandwich?

DANIEL. Okay.

(pause)

*(**WALT** moves into the kitchen.)*

WALT. You like anything in particular? I have turkey, roast beef –

DANIEL. Whatever's fine.

WALT. Well what would you like?

DANIEL. Whatever.

*(**WALT** comes out of the kitchen.)*

WALT. I know that this must be uncomfortable for you. And I'm sorry about – , there are usually many more people here, at times we've had nine or ten people staying in here at one time, some summers we had as many as thirty boys come through here. But I really want to make you comfortable, and safe, it's *important* to me that you feel safe. For the next few weeks, this is your home.

(pause)

DANIEL. I don't like roast beef.

WALT. So turkey?

DANIEL. Whatever.

WALT. I think there's baloney.

DANIEL. Turkey.

> (**WALT** *goes back into the kitchen, makes sandwiches.* **DANIEL** *tentatively sits down.*)

WALT. There are some really beautiful hiking trails we can do together, or if you just want to do them by yourself that's fine, I just ask that you don't go further than the ridge there if you're by yourself. There's a great lake you can get to but it's a day's hike. I don't know if I could make it that far, I'm –. But once Tim and Abby come, maybe they'd like to take you.

DANIEL. Tim and Abby?

WALT. Yeah, they –. Didn't your mom explain this to you?

DANIEL. She didn't –. She didn't tell me a lot.

WALT. Oh.

> *(pause)*

Well, they – they're friends, Abby helped me start this place, her husband Tim has been a counselor here for many years. And they'll be taking over this place once I –... Your mom really didn't explain this to you?

DANIEL. No.

> *(pause)*

WALT. You know there's candy in that jar in front of you if you want some – is there candy in there?

> (**DANIEL** *opens a candy jar on the coffee table in front of him.*)

DANIEL. Uh – yeah?

WALT. There's candy?

DANIEL. It's like – I think it's all tic tacs.

WALT. *Tic tacs?* I'll get some candy. *Tic tacs,* what is wrong with me?

DANIEL. So they're – your friends are coming here? To stay?

WALT. For a while, they'll help me pack up. And they'll be taking over this place next summer.

DANIEL. Are you moving?

(WALT finishes making a couple sandwiches, brings them out into the main room, hands one to DANIEL.)

WALT. I am. To an "assisted living center" or some other euphemism, "Shady Gardens" or "Garden Grove" or some other stupid thing. A place for people so old they fill their candy jars with tic tacs. I'm moving right after you finish up here.

DANIEL. So I'm your last – patient or whatever?

WALT. "Patient"? Are you sick?

DANIEL. Am I?

(pause)

WALT. You look fine and healthy to me.

(re: the sandwich)

Try it.

(DANIEL inspects the sandwich a bit.)

WALT. I didn't poison it, I promise.

DANIEL. What?

WALT. I'm kidding.

DANIEL. About *poisoning* me?

WALT. Alright, sorry, I'm –. Sorry?

(DANIEL pauses, then takes a bite of the sandwich.)

Okay?

(Pause. DANIEL nods.)

The good thing about being the only one here, you can have any room you like.

(DANIEL pulls out an iPhone.)

It can get a little cold at night, I'd rather you didn't use the space heater, I don't trust those things, I can give you a hot water bottle.

DANIEL. A what?

WALT. A hot water bottle, to sleep with, to keep you warm.

*(Pause. **DANIEL** looks at him.)*

DANIEL. You want me to sleep with a bottle full of warm water?

WALT. No, it's –. It's not like –

DANIEL. *(re: his iPhone)* There's no signal here?

WALT. Here? Heck no. I've heard when you walk up the ridge you can sometimes get, uh, signal. And there's a phone here. It's a rotary phone, you know how to use a rotary phone?

DANIEL. I don't know what that is.

WALT. Oh.

*(Awkward silence. **DANIEL** stares forward.)*

DANIEL. *(suddenly)* You're not gonna like *shock* me or anything, right?

WALT. "Shock" you? No, / we're –

DANIEL. Because you really don't need to do that, I don't –. Mom just sort of shoved me into a van without telling me anything, like *anything*, like *I don't even know your name*, and I read on the internet that sometimes people use electricity or whatever, / but I don't need that.

WALT. No one's going / to –

DANIEL. And why am I the only one here?! I really wasn't expecting to be the only one and I'm already feeling really uncomfortable, I can't even call anyone and you're making *jokes* about *poisoning me* –

WALT. I'm Walt. My name is Walt. Call me Walt.

(pause)

We don't shock anyone. We don't hurt you, we don't scold you, we don't try to beat you down. The only thing I've done, the only thing I've been trying to do for thirty years, is to raise you up. I know what you're feeling, you're feeling tired, confused, angry. I used to think I had it worse when I was a boy, but I'm convinced it's ten times harder nowadays, when all you have to do is open up a laptop and –.

(pause)

The first thing I want you to know, the first thing you need to know – you are safe here.

(pause)

You are safe here.

(pause)

DANIEL. So what are –? What are you going to do to me?

WALT. I'm not going to do anything "to you." We're going to talk, read scripture together, go on hikes, pray. I don't have any set curriculum here, this is all about you. Getting back to who you really are, the person you want to be.

DANIEL. A straight person.

(pause)

WALT. That's not really the best way to talk about it, it's not / about –

DANIEL. What if I told you I wasn't sure I wanted to be straight?

(pause)

WALT. It's your life, Daniel. I'm not here to force you into anything. Like I said, this is about you. Finding the person you've always wanted to be. It's a kind of baptism. But you have to, uh, make a decision about what kind of baptism – , what you're being baptized into. Ugh, that was stupid, I'm sorry. Forget I said that.

(pause)

What I think we should do now is – sit down and eat our sandwiches. I think that can be our start.

(pause)

Yeah?

Scene Two

(Several hours later. **ABBY** *stands in the middle of the room, holding a suitcase and some bags from Walmart.)*

ABBY. *(calling out)* Walt, you here?!

*(***TIM*** *appears in the hallway, entering the main room.)*

TIM. He's not in his bedroom.

*(***ABBY*** *goes to a window, looking out.)*

He knows we're coming today, right?

ABBY. Well he did when I talked to him yesterday, he –. Oh, it's terrible in here, get the windows?

*(***TIM*** *opens a couple windows.)*

ABBY. Where's that air conditioner we got for him?

TIM. He never liked that thing, it's probably sitting in the shed rusting over.

*(***ABBY*** *moves down the hall.)*

ABBY. *(offstage)* Well we paid enough for it, I don't –…

(short pause)

He's already packed up.

TIM. What?

*(***ABBY*** *re-enters.)*

ABBY. I said he's already packed up, I thought he said he wanted help packing.

TIM. Well it's not / completely –

ABBY. That road, I thought we were going to die. Those sheer drops on the passenger side on the way up, I had forgotten about those.

TIM. Better than it used to be.

ABBY. I'm still shaking. Where's that bottle of cognac?

*(***ABBY*** *goes to the kitchen, starts putting away the supplies in the Walmart bags.)*

TIM. We got it for Walt.

ABBY. Oh he won't mind, pour me a glass please?

(Pause. **TIM** *opens his bag, takes out a bottle of cognac.)*

TIM. Okay.

ABBY. Is it really that much trouble / to pour me a glass of –?

TIM. I'm doing it, honey, I'm pouring you a glass.

*(***TIM** *pours two drinks, brings one to* **ABBY.** *They drink.* **ABBY** *surveys the room, noticing a photo on the mantle. Pause.)*

TIM. What?

ABBY. No, I just –.

(pause)

I haven't been here in a while.

TIM. It feel different?

ABBY. Not at all. Looks exactly like it did in the beginning, it –…

(short pause)

I just hope Walt doesn't give me any grief, I have a feeling he's not too excited about going to the home.

TIM. You know, you really shouldn't call it "the home." Not in front of him at least.

ABBY. Oh who cares? It's a home, I'll call it a home if I want to.

TIM. I just – I don't think he'll like that, sounds like we're sending him off to an asylum.

*(***ABBY** *goes back to the Walmart bags, unpacking them.)*

ABBY. Well he's already given them the deposit, it's done. And the time has come, when he fell down last year, if Janet hadn't've stopped by that afternoon, I don't know what –

(rooting through the bag)

You got boat twine? Why did you get boat twine?

TIM. I just don't want him to feel like we're up here to send him off / on some iceberg or something.

ABBY. *(still rooting through the bag)* Well he knows we –… "Iceberg?" What the heck are you –?

(re: the bag) And *duct tape?* Tim, why on earth did you / buy this?

TIM. Oh I don't know, I just bought / some supplies –

ABBY. Are we helping him pack or taking him hostage?

(Pause. **TIM** *sits down.)*

TIM. I just –.

(pause)

It's just sad to see this place go.

*(***ABBY*** *regards the room.)*

ABBY. Sure.

(The door opens and **WALT** *enters.)*

WALT. Oh – / Hi –

TIM. *(getting up)* Well there he is!

*(***TIM*** *gets up, goes to* **WALT***, embracing him.)*

ABBY. Hello, Walter.

TIM. Where did you disappear off to?

WALT. Oh, I was just –. I was just out –…

*(***WALT*** *disappears down the hall.* **ABBY** *and* **TIM** *look at one another.)*

ABBY. Walt?

WALT. *(offstage)* Just, uh –. Sorry.

*(***WALT*** *returns.)*

Sorry! Good to see you. Uh – Daniel isn't here, is he?

TIM. Daniel?

WALT. Yeah, uh –. The boy, was there a boy here?

TIM. No –

ABBY. Wait – you don't have a kid up here, do you?

(pause)

WALT. Well, I just –. I know it's sort of last minute, but / he really –

ABBY. *(exasperated)* Walt, what were you / thinking?!

WALT. I'm sorry, I just –. His mother called me a few days ago, I / just thought –

ABBY. You're supposed to be moving into that place *next week*, they / have your –

WALT. They can wait an extra week or two, I'm still paying / for it –

TIM. You really think this is the best time for –?

WALT. Now listen, I'm sorry I didn't tell you, but –. But he's here, and he needs our help.

TIM. So – where is he?

WALT. Well see this is the, uh. I – don't really know.

ABBY. You don't know?

WALT. Well, he – he said something as he was leaving, he was at the door here, and he said something to me and I just, I can't remember what it was, but –. Ugh, I hate this, I hate it when I can't remember, I hear people saying things and the words travel in one ear / and out the –

ABBY. How long has he been gone?

WALT. Well, I don't know, what time is it?

TIM. *(checking his watch)* It's – almost six?

WALT. Oh.

TIM. When did he leave?

WALT. I guess it was around, uh. I don't know, noon?

(pause)

I guess I've been wandering around outside calling after him for about four hours now, I guess, I really lost track of time, uh.

(pause)

WALT. *(cont.)* Should we be concerned?

(pause)

Maybe we should be concerned.

Scene Three

(Later, nearly dark outside. WALT *is standing in the kitchen on the phone,* TIM *and* ABBY *have opened a few boxes and are rooting around inside them.)*

WALT. *(on the phone)* – well, yeah, I'm not –

(pause)

Wait, what? No, Janet, you're not – you're not understanding me, he's not *missing,* / he just went wandering outside or –

TIM. I'm not finding anything.

ABBY. *(to* WALT*)* You didn't label any of these, / I don't –

WALT. *(to* ABBY*)* Try the – oh, I don't know. Open the –

(on the phone)

No. Janet, I don't want the – you know, I don't want people thinking / that we *lost* him for gosh sake –

ABBY. He lives in a *cabin* in the *woods* and he doesn't own a *flashlight?*

WALT. *(on the phone)* I understand that, I really do, but this isn't – it's only been a few hours, I don't know if it's time to, you know, call in the National / Guard or whathaveyou.

TIM. Do we have something in the car?

ABBY. No.

WALT. *(on the phone)* Can't you just – / I don't know, ride around yourself, look for him a bit? Listen, if he's not back in a few hours, I'll be the first one to, you know, call Search and Rescue.

TIM. What about the little –

ABBY. We haven't had that for years.

TIM. What about the flares?

ABBY. *Flares?*

TIM. I was just thinking / that I –

ABBY. It hasn't rained here in three weeks and you wanna walk around in the forest here with *flares?*

WALT. *(on the phone)* / Yes, exactly, that's what I'm –. Yes, thank you, yes.

TIM. I just thought he might, the kid might see them or something. Nevermind.

ABBY. You're such a city boy.

TIM. You know I really don't like it when you call me that, Spokane isn't exactly / New York City –

ABBY. Oh I'm / just kidding, nevermind.

WALT. *(on the phone)* Okay, great. Thank you, Janet, and –. Yes, I appreciate the, uh. Discretion. Thank you.

(WALT hangs up.)

WALT. She's gonna, uh. She'll take a ride around, some of the old logging trails, see if she spots him.

TIM. Should we call his parents?

WALT. I just don't want to blow this out of proportion, we've dealt with this before –

TIM. I'm sure it's fine, but maybe we / should –

WALT. Let's just – not alarm too many people right now, alright? If he doesn't show up, you know, in a few hours, then we'll get worried.

TIM. So if he's not back in a couple hours, we call Janet back.

WALT. Yeah, of course.

TIM. For sure if he's not back by / midnight –

WALT. *Yes I heard you yes.*

(pause)

Maybe I shouldn't have done this, maybe I –. His mother was just so – *desperate.* She's already sent him to five or six different pastors –

TIM. Maybe you have a flashlight / out in the shed, or maybe –

WALT. Most of them sounded completely clueless, nowadays I'm not / even sure –

ABBY. Walt.

WALT. Hm?

ABBY. Flashlight.

WALT. Oh. *(pause)* Oh you know I think there's one in that closet there.

ABBY. *Geez*, Walt.

*(**WALT** goes to the closet, finds the flashlight.)*

WALT. Here just give me a minute, let me figure out where I put my coat and I'll go with you –

ABBY. Walt, just let Tim go, stay here with me.

WALT. He doesn't even know who Tim is, for all you know you might scare him away –

TIM. He's not a frightened deer, he's cold and thirsty and he'll be glad to see / another person –

WALT. Now Tim just give me a second, I said I can go with you.

TIM. *Walt, you'd slow me down.*

*(Pause. **WALT** looks away, hands **TIM** the flashlight.)*

WALT. Okay.

TIM. I didn't mean for that to / sound –

WALT. No, you're right, I'm –. I'd slow you down.

(pause) I should be here if he comes back anyway.

TIM. Sure.

(heading to the door)

Chances are he didn't go too far up the ridge, so I'll just head east a bit. He'll probably see my flashlight, come running.

WALT. Sure.

TIM. I won't go too far.

ABBY. Just watch where you're going, you're gonna / twist your ankle again if you don't watch where you're going –

TIM. I will. I said I will.

*(**TIM** kisses **ABBY** on the cheek, exits. A silence between **ABBY** and **WALT**.)*

ABBY. Walt, you really could have told us if you were planning on taking / on –

WALT. *Yes, I –*. I know. Abby, I've already said that I'm sorry, / I don't –

ABBY. Alright, alright, I'll –. I'll stop, I'm stopping.

(*pause*)

Look, I'm sure he's fine.

WALT. Sure.

ABBY. He's an Idaho kid, he'll be fine.

WALT. Mm-hm.

(*pause*)

ABBY. You didn't have to pack everything up by yourself, that's why we're here, you know.

WALT. I don't know, I just – wanted to get it all out of sight. Thought it'd make me feel better.

ABBY. Did it?

(*pause*)

WALT. No. No it, uh.

(**ABBY** *sits with* **WALT.**)

ABBY. On the way up here I was thinking about all those trips we did from town after we bought this place from the Boy Scouts. That time you were bringing the chest freezer up here, almost ran the pickup off the road.

WALT. I did not.

ABBY. You almost killed us both.

WALT. Oh that's such an exaggeration. And it wasn't the chest freezer, it was the stove.

ABBY. It was the freezer. I remember because you bought it from that Chinaman who ran the car dealership, you remember.

WALT. You know we're not supposed to say that now.

ABBY. What?

WALT. "Chinaman." It's racist or something.

ABBY. It's where he was from!

WALT. I know it, I didn't realize either. I used it a few years ago, one of the boys told me I shouldn't use the word, that it's insensitive.

ABBY. I don't even know what to say to that, it's where he's *from*. People are such idiots nowadays.

(They share a little laugh.)

WALT. It's nice to see you both. I'm sorry you had to have this drama the moment you got here.

ABBY. Any minute now Tim will walk in that door with him. We can focus on getting you ready to go to the home.

WALT. I wish you wouldn't call it that, "the home."

ABBY. Oh, Tim got on me for saying that too. I just don't care. I'm gonna say "the home" and "Chinaman" if I dang well want to, they're my words.

(pause)

Are you –…? I mean, how are you – feeling about it?

(pause)

WALT. Had to happen sooner or later. I can hide up here in the mountains from everything but death.

ABBY. Geez, Walt.

WALT. I'm not trying to be dark, I just –. It's fine, it's God's will. There's a pool.

(pause)

I'm just glad you two are taking over this place.

(Silence.)

ABBY. Walt, you know we –. You know Tim and I aren't getting any younger either, right?

WALT. Well, yeah. / What?

ABBY. It's just –. You have to realize, we have lives in Coeur d'Alene. I don't know if we can just pick everything up and move here for three months out of the year.

WALT. Wait, you –? What are you saying?

ABBY. Look, I didn't mean to bring this up immediately, but might as well just get it out there, no use keeping it from you.

WALT. You're not going to keep this place going?

ABBY. Okay, I never told you I would keep this place going, we never said that. It's not like we can just put our lives on hold for three months every year –

WALT. Well then I can hire people! If you / two don't –

ABBY. *Hire* people? Walt, where the heck would we get money to hire a staff? You only brought four kids up here last summer, and two of them you didn't even *charge* anything –

WALT. Okay, Abby –

ABBY. And your rest home isn't *free*, you know? Tim said that even some of the cheaper units can cost five thousand a month, and I know that you don't –… *Darn it*, I don't know why I have to be the one to do this, I don't know why I always have to be the adult.

(WALT gets up, wandering aimlessly.)

(silence)

(ABBY softens, goes to him.)

Walt, you've done – good work. Great work. But you said yourself, this is God's will. You have to move on.

(WALT looks at her.)

WALT. And next year, when there's another boy, another ten boys, who are confused, and suffering, and alone, where are they gonna go? What's out there for them? How many more boys are gonna end up like –…?

(Pause. ABBY gets up, looking around for a moment. She finds her purse, roots around in it.)

WALT. I'm sorry.

ABBY. No, I'm –. Look I'm just thinking I could drive around a bit to see if I see / anything –

WALT. I said I'm sorry, I / didn't –

ABBY. There's no reason I shouldn't be out there looking for him as well, I'll just –.

(**ABBY** *heads toward the door.*)

WALT. Abby, wait.

(**ABBY** *stops, not looking at* **WALT.***)

Isaac died because he didn't have a place like this. I just want you to remember that.

(**ABBY** *looks at* **WALT.** *Silence.*)

ABBY. I'll come right back if I find him.

(*Pause.* **ABBY** *exits.*)

Scene Four

(Later that night. **TIM**, *having just walked in the door, watches a DVD that has been left playing on the television.* **WALT** *is at a table, having fallen asleep.)*

VOICEOVER ON THE TELEVISION. – only one mile away, which was awarded a Medicare rating of 83 out of 100. Residents can choose from private condominiums, located only steps away from the golf course, or bedrooms in our Cottage House, a fourteen unit assisted living center for senior citizens with physical or mental difficulties.

*(***TIM*** approaches ***WALT***, reaching a hand out toward his shoulder.)*

Visit us at Shady Grove and you'll find our residents happy, alert, groomed, well-fed, and healthy. You'll find our staff caring, / friendly, jovial, and speaking with attention to speed and volume.

WALT. *(startled)* OH –

TIM. Sorry! Sorry –

WALT. Tim, you really almost just killed me –

TIM. I'm sorry.

VOICEOVER ON THE TELEVISION. / Amenities include a hair salon, bank, gift shop, snack wagon, gym facilities, pool, and library. We also offer regular shuttles to many popular shopping destinations, as well as some of the best restaurants the Treasure Valley has to offer.

TIM. He hasn't come back yet?

WALT. No, you didn't see anything?

TIM. No, I – I went toward the lake, almost as far as the dead forest, I didn't see anything. You're sure he went that way? He didn't go back down the road?

WALT. I don't – I have no idea. He said something, then he was gone.

TIM. You *really* don't remember what he said?

WALT. Tim, if I knew what he said, don't you think I'd *tell you?*

TIM. Alright, alright. Is Abby out looking for him?

WALT. Yeah, she's –. She's driving around a bit.

*(Pause. **WALT** paces nervously, looks out a window. **TIM** looks at the television.)*

VOICEOVER ON THE TELEVISION. Every day offers our residents new activities such as crafting, sing-along, reading, monthly communal birthday parties, / cocktail hour, church services, and art classes.

TIM. Is that –?

WALT. What?

TIM. On the TV. That's where you're going?

WALT. Oh, the –. Yeah.

VOICEOVER ON THE TELEVISION. Almost every hallway in Shady Grove prominently displays art by our residents, / like these seen here. Our art teachers are highly trained professionals who have years of experience with –

TIM. It looks nice.

WALT. Mm-hm.

TIM. Art classes, that's –

*(***WALT** turns off the television. Short pause. **TIM** heads toward the door.)*

TIM. I'm gonna head back out, I just wanted to make sure he didn't come back. I'm wondering if he took the trail up around the other side of the ridge, maybe / he –

WALT. Tim, Abby told me –. She told me that you're not taking over this place.

*(***TIM** stops. Pause.)*

TIM. Listen, I –. I want you to know that I really don't want to see this place close down, I tried to convince her that we could keep it running –

WALT. Mm-hm.

TIM. But you know Abby. She's been talking about you selling this place for at least five years now.

WALT. She has?

TIM. We argued about it the whole way here. I mean when was the last time she spent more than a few nights here? Six, seven years ago? Last summer she didn't want me coming up at all.

(pause)

Listen, even if this place doesn't shut down – that doesn't mean we're giving up. I'm still counseling boys out of my office, I've one I'm working with right now. And you can always come up to Couer d'Alene to work with me – you could even do some counseling in Boise part time, I could come down a few weeks out of the year to work with you, or –...

(pause)

Point is – this isn't over.

(pause)

WALT. It's an interesting feeling.

TIM. What?

WALT. I don't know. Becoming a dinosaur.

(pause)

TIM. Wait – what do you mean?

(Headlights shine through the window, the sound of an approaching car.)

WALT. Is that Abby?

(TIM *opens the door, looking out.)*

TIM. No, it's –. I don't know.

(Sound of a car door closing.)

(calling out)

Hello?

(After a moment, **EUNICE** *appears at the door. She looks at* **TIM** *for a second, then* **WALT**, *not saying anything.)*

TIM. Can we –...?

*(***EUNICE** *pushes past* **TIM**, *goes inside.)*

Excuse me?

*(***EUNICE** *looks around, then heads down the hall.)*

Do you know who that is?

WALT. I have no –...

EUNICE. *(offstage)* Danny?!

WALT. Oh.

*(***EUNICE** *re-enters.)*

EUNICE. Where is he?

WALT. Well, we actually –

EUNICE. I got a text from him, I tried calling him back but he wouldn't answer, and the phone number you gave me for this place has been busy for hours. Where is he?

WALT. Oh that phone –

*(***WALT** *goes to the phone, looking at it.)*

It's this stupid old rotary / phone –

EUNICE. *Where's Daniel?*

WALT. Okay, okay, just –. I'm Walt, we spoke on the phone. It's Eunice, right?

(pause)

EUNICE. Yes.

WALT. Eunice. Daniel went out for a walk this afternoon, he hasn't come back yet. But we'll find him, / I promise you –

EUNICE. Oh Lord please no –

TIM. It's really not as bad as it sounds –

EUNICE. Oh Lord, oh Lord / please no –

WALT. Sit down, please –

> (**EUNICE** *sits down on the couch.*)

TIM. Chances are he'll come back later tonight or –… He's probably not even lost, he might just be – I mean, you know how teenage boys can be, they can pull these kinds of things –

EUNICE. Not Daniel. Daniel doesn't do this.

TIM. You'd be surprised at what they're capable of, even the ones you / don't –

EUNICE. I'm sorry, who are you?

WALT. He works here, with me. And we've dealt with this kind of thing –

EUNICE. So what are you doing, have you called the police, the – I don't know – *ranger*, or –

WALT. There's a ranger here who's a good friend, has been for years, she's aware of it, she's on the lookout. If we don't hear from her in a few hours we'll make some more calls. Really, I know how stressful this must be but honestly – it's going to be okay.

TIM. What did the text say?

EUNICE. What?

TIM. You said he texted you?

EUNICE. Oh. Yeah.

TIM. What did it say?

EUNICE. It said "I'm gone."

> (*pause*)

It just said "I'm gone."

Scene Five

(Later that night, around midnight.)

(JANET, *a park ranger, is standing in the cabin with an open notebook.)*

(WALT, **TIM**, **ABBY**, *and* **EUNICE** *sit in various places around the cabin.)*

JANET. I tell you, you could drive for *eight hours* and not see another living soul. *Hundreds* of miles. Or "kilometers" or whatever shit. I'm telling you, Australia – that's some *real* wilderness. Makes this all seem like a city park. My husband and I spent a couple weeks out there, and I can / tell you –

TIM. Janet –

JANET. I'm just saying! You shouldn't be too worried. If he was lost out in the Outback, that's when you'd have to be worried. Plus they have these dingos.

ABBY. So what should we be doing? Is there anything that we / can –

JANET. I mean listen, you guys know how it goes, you've seen this before. Chances are he's already ran into some hikers, this time of year it's damn near impossible not to run into anyone after this long.

    (to **EUNICE***)* Honey, you have *nothing* to worry about.

EUNICE. I'm sorry?

JANET. I'm saying, honey, you have nothing to worry about. This kind of situation happens once every couple years, not a single one has died on us yet.

EUNICE. Oh.

TIM. *Janet.*

ABBY. Alright, there has to be something *we* can do?

JANET. Wouldn't hurt to do some driving around, honk the horn a bit. Maybe he found one of the old logging roads, could be following that. Lemme get you a map, we made new ones last year.

(JANET *fishes around in one of her oversized pockets, pulls out a map.*)

JANET. *(cont.)* They're pretty nice now. Used satellites to make 'em, accurate as hell. If you guys wanna drive around, you never know. But honestly, my guess is by now he's run into some hikers, they're probably takin' him to the trail head right now. This reminds me of that one kid from ten years back or so? Remember that?

WALT. Uh.

JANET. The fat little shit from Twin Falls, got lost on one of Walt's nature hikes, wandered around for hours before he ran into that group on horseback or something –

ABBY. Okay, I can do some driving around – Tim, you can head toward the lake again?

TIM. Sure. Walt, you'll stick around here in case he comes back?

(WALT *doesn't respond, lost in thought.*)

Walt.

WALT. Hm? Oh, yeah, I'll –. I'll stay here.

(pause)

TIM. Maybe you should get a little sleep?

WALT. I'm fine.

TIM. There's no use in sitting around / worrying –

WALT. *I said I'm fine, Tim, I –.*

(pause)

If you find him, come right back, okay?

TIM. Sure.

(TIM *and* ABBY *both leave.*)

JANET. Okay! Now it's, uh – Eunice? Is that right?

EUNICE. Yes.

JANET. Pretty name.

EUNICE. Okay.

JANET. So it might help if I ask you a few questions, you feel up for that?

EUNICE. Yeah, of course.

JANET. Now just so I know, does your son have any wilderness training under his belt?

EUNICE. Wilderness training?

JANET. You know, was he a Boy Scout, did he go camping, you know –?

EUNICE. He was a Cub Scout. He quit when he was a –, what do you call it, Webelos?

JANET. Okay so he has some training then.

EUNICE. I don't think so. They mostly went bowling.

JANET. Fun! What about camping, would he have any skills along those lines?

EUNICE. He went camping a few times, I don't know. He hated it, I know that much.

JANET. Well anything you can tell us about / his –

EUNICE. Why does this matter, I don't –?

JANET. Well see the thing is, if we know he has some training, experience, we're gonna be better informed about where to look. If he even has some basic knowledge of wilderness survival, that might help us track him, whereas if he really doesn't know anything –

EUNICE. He doesn't know anything. You should treat this – situation like he doesn't know anything.

JANET. Okay! Now it doesn't get too cold at night this time of year, but just in case, was he wearing something warm when he left?

WALT. Yeah, he had –. I think it was – , was it like a – hooded sweatshirt?

JANET. So he had some layers on / then?

EUNICE. He doesn't own any hoodies.

WALT. I remember it was this, green? No, / it –

EUNICE. Shorts and a blue tee-shirt, a tan jacket – if he was wearing it?

WALT. Yes, he – that sounds right. I think that sounds right. I'm sorry.

JANET. It's okay! Now did he say anything to you before he left, anything / about –?

WALT. No see that's just the thing, I can't remember what he –… I mean he did say something, I'm sure he said something to me, and I remember nodding or smiling, and then he left –

JANET. So you can't remember what he said? Maybe just really think about it.

WALT. I *am* really thinking about it. I really just –. I don't remember, I'm sorry.

JANET. Maybe if you think of it you could maybe give me a call, just if you think of it.

WALT. Yeah, I –. Yeah, of course.

(**EUNICE** *starts laughing softly to herself.*)

JANET. You okay honey?

(pause)

EUNICE. This is so –… This is ridiculous. This is *so ridiculous.*

WALT. / Okay –

JANET. / Honey –

EUNICE. You people are –… I just can't stand your – *attitude* toward this, you come in here and you ask me if he was a *Boy Scout*, you can't even remember what he was wearing, or *what he said to you* –

JANET. *(surprisingly stern)* Ma'am you're gonna have to take it down a notch right now.
(pause) Now there's a few things you need to understand here. I've known this man here for damn near eighteen years, and I can tell you that he cares for each of these boys like they were his own.

EUNICE. Fine, but that's not the whatever, *issue* right now, the issue is neither of you even seem *alarmed* about this –

JANET. You'd rather I freak out, go nuts, scream my head off?

EUNICE. No, I just –

JANET. I want you to know that I take this very seriously. Two summers ago, we had two hikers go missing. First eighteen hours, I wasn't too concerned. Vast majority of the time, people turn up within eighteen hours. But these guys, they didn't show up. So I dialed it up. I called up Search and Rescue, organized search parties on my own, got a friend of mine to take his helicopter up to do some rounds. Found them within four hours. They were thirsty and scared, but they were fine.

(pause)

My gut tells me your son is gonna be just fine, so right now I'm very calm about this whole thing. But believe me, if we get to the point where I need to dial it up, then believe me I'm gonna dial it up.

(pause)

EUNICE. Okay.

JANET. Okay! Now is there anything else you think might be relevant? I don't suppose he's ever been up here before, he wouldn't have any relationship to the area, would he?

(pause)

EUNICE. Well, he –. Yeah, he was up here once.

JANET. Oh yeah?

EUNICE. Yeah, his, uh –. His dad took him up here, couple years ago.

JANET. Close by here?

EUNICE. I mean, I don't know.

JANET. Could you maybe call up your husband and find out where it might have been roughly?

EUNICE. No, I couldn't.

(pause)

JANET. Okay then. Well I think I'm about done here. I just wanna make sure that someone stays here, at all times, there's a good chance that he's just gonna come straight back here to the cabin.

WALT. Sure.

(*JANET puts away her notebook, heads to the door,* **WALT** *walks with her.*)

Thanks, Janet.

JANET. Sure thing. When are you gonna be heading out by the way?

WALT. Uh, soon. Fairly soon, few weeks.

JANET. Well you gotta be sure and let Clint and I cook you dinner before you take off, okay?

WALT. Yeah, uh. Sure.

(*pause*)

Thanks.

(*JANET exits.* **WALT** *closes the door behind her. He turns to* **EUNICE.**)

Does his, uh. Is Daniel's father – does he know what's going on?

(*pause*)

EUNICE. He's fine.

WALT. You don't think he'd want to know?

EUNICE. To be honest Dennis probably wouldn't want to know. He wouldn't come up here, anyway.

(*EUNICE gets up, looks for her coat.*)

Okay, I can't stand this, I'm going to go out there and look for him myself –

WALT. Now, really, that's not a / good idea –

EUNICE. I'm not just going to sit here and chat while my / son is out there *in complete darkness* –

WALT. Really Janet is much more qualified to be / handling these situations –

EUNICE. *Well I don't know what to do, I have no clue what to –...*

> **(EUNICE** *stops, becoming upset. She looks away from* **WALT.** *Short pause.)*

WALT. I understand the instinct, if I was ten years younger I'd be out there screaming his name myself. But there's no use in getting another person lost out in those woods. Honestly, the best thing we can do for him right now – is pray for him. Pray for him to *come back.*

> **(WALT** *goes to* **EUNICE.)**

Will you pray with me?

> **(EUNICE** *looks at* **WALT.** *Pause.)*

EUNICE. I don't –...

WALT. What?

EUNICE. I don't know, maybe I shouldn't have sent him here, maybe –... I mean, so he looked at a few videos on the internet, so what? You never glanced at a dirty magazine when you were a kid?

> *(pause)*

WALT. Listen, I've dealt with this quite a lot, these things can get out of control pretty quickly. Nowadays, with the kids growing up with these computers, it's all too easy to find.

> *(pause)*

EUNICE. So what did you –... You didn't *do* anything to him, did you?

WALT. What?

EUNICE. I mean I don't really know what goes on up here, I – I mean you didn't do anything weird, you didn't *shock* him, / or –?

WALT. *No,* I didn't –. Why does everyone think I *shock* people? We talked about this on the phone, I sent you all our literature –

EUNICE. Dennis always reads the literature, I didn't look. And I tried not to listen when we talked on the phone.

WALT. Why?

EUNICE. Dennis has sent him to so many pastors, weekend workshops, but this time –. Sending him up here, for weeks up in the woods, I –. I honestly didn't want to know what you –…

(pause)

WALT. It's just – talking, mostly. Talking, praying, reading scripture.

EUNICE. Well it's a nicer approach than Dennis had, I'll give you that.

(Pause. WALT looks at EUNICE.)

WALT. Pray with me?

(After a moment, EUNICE and WALT bow their heads.)

EUNICE. Dear Lord, I –…

(pause)

Please keep Daniel safe out there, please –. Please find it in your wisdom to bring him back to –…

(pause)

Please just let him find some stream to drink out of, let him find some berries or something to eat. Maybe a cozy little cave to sleep in? Maybe just make it nice for him out there, maybe –…

(WALT raises his head, looking at EUNICE.)

(EUNICE pauses briefly, then continues.)

Maybe it's really nice for him out there, maybe he's happy. Maybe he's –…

(EUNICE stops, opening her eyes. Pause. WALT attempts to continue the prayer.)

WALT. And Lord, we ask that you –

EUNICE. Do you think that someone like Daniel, do you think they can really – change?

(pause)

I mean *you* changed, right?

(**WALT** *looks at her, doesn't respond. Silence.*)

I'm sorry, I just assumed that you –

WALT. Yes, I –. Many years ago I did – struggle with it.

EUNICE. And how did you – get rid of it?

WALT. If you don't mind, / I'd rather not –

EUNICE. Walt, I don't know if you can tell but I'm sort of at the end of my rope here, I –...

(pause)

I need someone to tell me that this can work.

(pause)

WALT. You know for thirty years parents have been asking me that, they want some reassurance that it *will work*, and –...

(pause)

Just before I graduated high school, there was another boy in my class who I was – close with. We carried on for nearly a year before –...

(pause)

He had started going to this park, this place in Boise where men like him would go to find each other. Somehow his parents found out what was going on, and they sent him to some psychiatrist who would do those electro-shock therapies you were so worried about.

(pause)

I was – terrified, I didn't know where to turn, so I sought out a church. A nice pastor named Clark took me under his wing. He made me realize – the problem was in *me*, there was something in *me* that wasn't right. And I needed to conquer it.

EUNICE. And it worked? You actually – changed?

(pause)

WALT. For me, it –. Yes, I –...

(**WALT** *looks away, his eyes glazing over. Silence.*)

EUNICE. What happened to him?

WALT. Pastor Clark? Oh, he died years ago –

EUNICE. No, the –. Your friend. The boy.

(pause)

WALT. I don't know.

(pause)

EUNICE. What was his name?

(Long silence. **WALT** *stares forward.)*

Are you okay?

(pause)

WALT. I don't remember. It doesn't matter, anyway.

(**WALT** *bows his head, praying.* **EUNICE** *watches him, not bowing her head.*)

Dear Lord, we ask that you return Daniel to us. We ask that you keep him safe, and return him back to us. In Christ's name we pray.

(short pause)

Amen.

(**EUNICE** *continues to watch him.*)

Scene Six

(Later that night. EUNICE *watches the Shady Grove DVD from before. Most of the lights in the cabin are off.)*

VOICEOVER ON THE TELEVISION. It's about relating to people as people, not just patients. It's about making real connections with each of our residents. Our employees cherish life for the remarkable journey that it has been, and is still to come.

*(***ABBY*** enters from outside.)*

/ As one of Boise's oldest providers of senior care, we've had a lot of experience.

ABBY. *(calling out)* Tim?!

EUNICE. He's not back yet.

ABBY. That stupid car is overheating again, he knows what to –…

*(***ABBY*** sees ***EUNICE*** watching the television. She stops.)*

ABBY. Are you –…? You doing okay?

VOICEOVER ON THE TELEVISION. Assisted living communities provide or coordinate oversight and –

*(***ABBY*** turns off the television.)*

(An uncomfortable silence.)

ABBY. You know if you wanted to get some rest, I'd be happy to stay here in case –

EUNICE. No, I –. There's no way I could sleep.

(pause)

So you and Tim, you're – counselors here, or whatever?

(pause)

ABBY. Tim more than me nowadays, but – yeah.

(pause)

I was here at the beginning.

EUNICE. So Walt and you – the two of you founded this place?

ABBY. A long time ago, yes.

(pause)

When we were married.

*(Pause. **EUNICE** looks at **ABBY**.)*

EUNICE. Oh.

(pause)

I don't mean to –.... In my church, divorce doesn't really exist.

ABBY. Well it didn't exist in ours either, it –.

(pause)

It was a very difficult time.

(pause)

EUNICE. I just –. I hate myself for just sitting around, I should be out there shouting his name at the top of my lungs... But I'm not doing that. Why am I not doing that?

(pause)

ABBY. You're exhausted. You're exhausted and stressed. Every mother thinks she's terrible at it at some point.

*(Pause. **ABBY** joins **EUNICE**.)*

EUNICE. I grew up in this beautiful little town in northern Wyoming, about three hundred people? And we all knew each other, and we all went to the same church, and everything always just – *made sense.* Then I met Dennis at Bible college, he started his own church and it became one of the biggest in the state, and we had a baby, and it all –. God had given me a life that made sense. But Danny –...

(pause)

Ever since he was old enough to talk, he's always been so – *feminine.* All his friends were girls, he was never interested in sports, or –. So Dennis would take him on these camping trips, these camping trips that he thought would somehow *help*, or –. And when he caught Danny on the computer that day, Dennis just –... I'd never seen him like that. It just – didn't make sense. To either of us.

(pause)

And from then on, Dennis just – *refused* to interact with him. Mostly he'd just hide him away. When you're running a church you don't really want your feminine little secret running around and –...

(pause)

Maybe we should just let him be. Maybe he should just move out when he's eighteen, find some life within it. Maybe that's better for everyone.

*(Pause. **ABBY** goes to **EUNICE.**)*

ABBY. Our son Isaac – he was like that. I mean it wasn't obvious like that, we didn't get much of an idea of it before he –.

(pause)

I take that back, we had an idea of it. Walt and I both had an idea of it, we just didn't want to – say it out loud, I guess. And one night, Isaac had a boy over from his class, and I walk into their room in the morning, and they're – *on* one another.

(pause)

So we scolded him, we read scripture at him, sent him to church camps. And he tried and tried, but nothing seemed to work, nothing seemed to kick it out of him. We finally just said – there's nothing we can do. Just let him leave town, make a life. A life lived in sin, but –.

(pause)

Four months later, Isaac hanged himself in his apartment. His landlord found him. His landlord that he barely knew.

(**ABBY** *looks at* **EUNICE.** *Pause.*)

EUNICE. I –

ABBY. This is what you *have to understand* – this isn't just about temptation, or sexual immorality. We all sin, we all fall short of perfection and need forgiveness. But when you allow him to *accept* that part of himself, to embrace it, when you allow him to give up the fight – then you quietly *damn* him. This isn't about his life here on earth – better he spend *every moment* fighting that part of himself than surrender to death in this life *and* the next.

(*Pause.* **ABBY** *takes* **EUNICE**'s *hand, becoming upset.* **EUNICE** *is frozen.*)

So when you say to yourself that it might be better to let him go, try to make a life within it? You remember there is *no life within that.* Remember my son, Isaac.

(*The front door opens,* **TIM** *enters.*)

TIM. I didn't see anything, couldn't even –…

(*seeing* **ABBY**)

What?

ABBY. Nothing. The car is overheating again, / can you –?

TIM. What's wrong?

(**EUNICE** *gets up, goes to a window, looking outside, lost in thought.*)

ABBY. Nothing, I was just –. I'm fine.

TIM. What are you upset about?

ABBY. I said I'm fine, don't –. Just leave it alone.

(**WALT** *enters from down the hall, just woken up.*)

WALT. Did either / of you –?

ABBY. No.

(**WALT** *looks at* **ABBY**.)

WALT. Is everything –?

(JANET *enters from outside. Unseen by the rest of the group,* EUNICE *starts to silently break down.*)

ABBY. / It's fine.

JANET. Sorry to, uh. Sorry to barge in, but things have just gotten a little more complicated out there.

WALT. What does that mean?

JANET. I just got a call from a look-out about forty miles south of here, some lightning just got a forest fire started –

WALT. Oh –

JANET. Don't know how big yet, but there haven't been many fires this season, so it could spread pretty quick.

(to WALT*)*

Listen I know you wanna keep this quiet, but I had to –...

(seeing EUNICE*)*

You okay there?

*(*EUNICE *collapses into herself.* ABBY *goes to her.*)

ABBY. *(going to* EUNICE*)* Okay, it's alright, just take a moment.

TIM. Is she / okay?

ABBY. She's fine. She just needs a moment.

JANET. *(to* WALT*)* What this means is the time has come to call in some other people here.

WALT. I just, I don't want to make this into a big scene –

JANET. I understand that, but –

TIM. We can't keep sitting on our hands here, / Walt –

WALT. I'm not sitting on my hands, / no one's – !

JANET. I already radioed the sheriff, Search and Rescue is on the / way here, they've –

WALT. Search and Rescue?! It's only / been –

JANET. Walt, I'm sorry, it's outta my hands now. It's done.

TIM. So what can we do?

JANET. Search and Rescue's gonna start moving all over the area, but I was thinkin' I could make some calls and start organizing some search parties on my own, so / we can –

WALT. *(losing himself)* *No, we are not –... I'm not having this turn into some sort of circus, I'm not –...*

*(****WALT*** *trails off, everyone falls silent.* ***WALT*** *looks away, sitting down.)*

(Silence.)

EUNICE. *(a half-prayer)* He's drinking from streams. He's eating berries. He's sleeping in warm little caves. He's fishing, and making fires at night.

(pause)

Right now he's – happy, he's looking up into the sky, right now. He's happy.

End of Act One

ACT TWO

Scene One

(Mid-day, around noon. **WALT** *and* **DANIEL** *sit on the couch, two plates with mostly eaten sandwiches sit on the coffee table in front of them.* **DANIEL***'s duffel bag sits near him on the couch.)*

*(***WALT*** is holding a purple heirloom tomato.)*

WALT. This is – ?

(pause)

What is it?

DANIEL. It's a tomato.

WALT. But it's purple.

DANIEL. It's an heirloom tomato.

WALT. "Heirloom"?

DANIEL. It's stupid. I'm just sort of into it. I know it's a weird thing to be into.

WALT. I'm into dictionaries and you're into tomatoes, we make a good team.

DANIEL. I just like them, they're not like regular tomatoes, they breed true.

WALT. And what does that mean?

DANIEL. It means like when you mate them with each other, they produce the same kind of tomato. Different than the hybridized tomatoes you buy at the store.

WALT. And you grow these in your backyard?

DANIEL. Mostly. Some in my room, too.

WALT. Are they – difficult to grow?

DANIEL. They're *really* difficult to grow. But I'm pretty good at it.

(DANIEL reaches into his backpack, pulls out another tomato wrapped in a cloth.)

DANIEL. This one's a Green Zebra.

(WALT takes the tomato, looking at it.)

WALT. How on earth did you become interested in this?

DANIEL. I don't know, I just like gardening.

WALT. Hm.

(pause)

DANIEL. Is that okay?

WALT. What do you mean?

DANIEL. Is it okay that I like to garden?

WALT. Why the heck wouldn't it be okay?

DANIEL. I don't know, I – . Dad sent me to a couple pastors, they both said I shouldn't do it. That it's a woman thing or –, something. I don't know.

WALT. Oh.

(pause)

People have probably told you some pretty – outlandish things about yourself.

DANIEL. This one guy I got sent to, in Colorado Springs, he said I was probably too close with my mother.

WALT. Are you?

DANIEL. I mean closer than I am to my dad, but not – . Not that close.

(pause)

WALT. A lot of things can happen, there are many things that can – contribute to this. It's usually pretty hard to figure out exactly where it came from.

DANIEL. Where do you think it comes from?

(WALT chuckles.)

WALT. You've only been here for less than an hour, Daniel, we don't have to get into the big questions so / quickly –

DANIEL. No, really. Where do you think it comes from?

(pause)

WALT. If I knew for certain it would make my job a lot easier.

(pause)

Sin is inherent from Adam. We're all born with it. Maybe – there isn't a concrete reason, maybe it's just something we have to overcome.

*(Pause. **DANIEL** takes out another tomato, hands it to **WALT.**)*

DANIEL. This one's called Aunt Ruby's German Green.

WALT. Wow.

DANIEL. It's a stupid name but it's a great tomato. Tastes really good when you pick it early.

WALT. So why did you – ? Why bring them all the way up here?

(pause)

DANIEL. I just – . I think my dad might dig them up when I'm gone. I just had a feeling.

(pause)

WALT. Well, we'll keep them safe for you. I'll put them in the fridge.

DANIEL. That's bad for them actually. Just put them in a paper bag if you have one.

*(**WALT** carefully takes the tomatoes, brings them to the kitchen, finds a paper bag and puts them inside.)*

WALT. There's a small garden outside. Might need some cleaning up but if you plant something now it might be ready by the time you leave. Something quick maybe.

DANIEL. That might be cool. You have seeds?

WALT. We can get some. We need to run into town before Tim and Abby get here, anyway. I think there's still a gardening center there. Or wait – did that close?

DANIEL. I can look it up. Do you have wifi, or – ?

(**DANIEL** *takes out his iPhone.*)

WALT. Oh, there's no internet at all up here.

(*pause*)

DANIEL. There's no – ?

WALT. No, sorry, but the phone book / is –

DANIEL. Is it because of me?

WALT. Is what because of you?

DANIEL. Did you get rid of the internet because of me?

(*Pause.* **WALT** *goes to* **DANIEL.**)

WALT. I've never had internet up here, I promise.

(*pause*)

How many times had you – looked at things on the internet like that?

(*pause*)

DANIEL. I mean not a lot.

WALT. Every day?

DANIEL. No, not like – . It was just once. Seriously. They caught me doing it the very first time I did it.

(*pause*)

WALT. Was it photos, or – ?

DANIEL. Do we have to talk about this? This is really embarrassing –

WALT. You have *nothing* to be embarrassed about. I want you to feel safe talking to me, about anything. I've been doing this for a while now, and I can't tell you how important it is to articulate what it is you're feeling. Once it's put into words, we can know what it is. Until then it's just this mass of confusion festering in your gut. If you put it into words – you can assess it. Control it.

(pause)

DANIEL. It was – . It was a video.

WALT. Of what?

(pause)

DANIEL. Like, two guys who were – . One guy like had the other guy – .

(Silence. **DANIEL** *looks away.)*

WALT. Was it oral sex or anal sex?

(pause)

Do you know what I'm talking about when I / say – ?

DANIEL. *Yeah* I know what – .

(pause)

Oral sex.

(pause)

WALT. How much of it did you watch?

DANIEL. Not a lot. Like a minute or so.

WALT. How did you feel? When you were watching it?

(pause)

DANIEL. Scared.

WALT. Good.

(pause)

That's good.

*(***WALT*** *sits down on the couch.)*

We can head into town later today, there's a few things we need anyway. We could actually do some grilling tonight if you like, I know Tim and Abby would like that, they're coming all the way here from Couer d'Alene, I'm sure they'll be hungry.

DANIEL. Do they – ? Are they going to be – talking with me too?

WALT. Well I'm sure they'll say hello.

DANIEL. You know what I mean.

WALT. No, they won't be counseling you, they're just coming up for a few nights. You want another sandwich?

DANIEL. I'm fine, thanks.

(pause)

So I'm like – the last one who's gonna come up here?

WALT. Well, last one while I'm still here. Tim and Abby will be taking it over next year. And I can still come up for part of the summer. And hopefully they'll pass it on eventually, maybe even someone like you will be running it someday.

DANIEL. So why did you – ? I mean what made you start it?

WALT. A lot of things, I suppose. I just know how hard it is, I know what it's like. My son Isaac dealt with it. That's the reason I wanted to start this in the first place.

DANIEL. Did he – ? He was able to – change?

(pause)

WALT. He was – never really given the chance.

(pause)

Back then, we didn't really know how to deal with it. We did what so many people still do today, we treated it like a disease that needed to be cured. We lectured him, took him to Bible studies, threw scripture at him, and after a while he – had enough. He left the house, moved away. What we never did was *listen* to him, make him feel safe, and just – *listen.* All I ever wanted was for him to feel safe. Even when he left, I told him that all I ever wanted was for him to feel safe.

(pause)

So I suppose this place is our small effort to make sure that boys like Isaac have a place where they can feel safe.

(pause)

DANIEL. What happened to him?

*(Pause. **WALT** looks at him.)*

WALT. Four months after leaving home, he was gone. In a studio apartment, alone. Just like that – he was gone.

*(Pause. **WALT** stands up.)*

Alright, I can let you get settled in before we make the run into town, like I said feel free to take whichever bedroom you like.

DANIEL. I think I might go for a walk?

WALT. Oh. That's – of course, that's fine. I can show you around if you like, there's a few / trails that –

DANIEL. I'd rather just – . If it's alright, I sorta just wanna be by myself.

(pause)

I won't go far.

WALT. Oh. Well that's – fine.

*(**DANIEL** heads toward the door, opening it.)*

(The sound of a fire begins to fill the space, growing in volume.)

*(**WALT** grabs the dishes, heads to the kitchen, puts them in the sink. **DANIEL** opens the door, then stops.)*

DANIEL. Walt?

WALT. Yeah?

*(**WALT** looks at **DANIEL.** The sound of the fire grows and grows until it's almost deafening.)*

(The lights snap to black, the fire continues for a few moments in darkness.)

(Slowly, we begin to hear the sound of a phone ringing as the fire subsides.)

Scene Two

(Lights rise on the cabin, just before dawn. **WALT** *has dragged a lamp next to the dictionary. He's squinting through the magnifying glass, trying to read. There is a small, dying fire in the fireplace.)*

(The phone rings again. **WALT** *ignores it for a while, then finally goes to the phone and answers it.* **TIM** *enters from outside, filthy and exhausted.*

WALT. Hello?

*(***WALT** *hangs up the phone.)*

TIM. Which one was that?

WALT. Oh, the – . I don't know, Spokane paper.

TIM. You're just hanging up on them now?

WALT. Well I tried talking to one of them from the – I don't know what paper it was, but she just asked me these leading questions. Still nothing?

TIM. Janet's got a couple search parties heading further north, Search and Rescue's bringing in helicopters from Montana.

(Short pause.)

WALT. It's really just awful, these journalists using this, *exploiting* this boy. They're probably having a great time with it. Anyway, if they want to blame me, then fine.

TIM. No one's blaming you. And I doubt Eunice and her husband would be, you know. Litigious about it. If they were, I could help you out.

*(***WALT** *makes his way back to the dictionary, picks up the magnifying glass, starts looking again.)*

WALT. You want to become known as the lawyer who defends old men who kill boys?

TIM. Stop it, Walt, he's not – . What are you looking for?

WALT. Oh, I'm just – . I just couldn't think of the word, this – this reporter, she was being so… *Devious*, you know. But not that word, that's not the right word. I wanted to tell her how she was being but I couldn't find the word.

TIM. "Duplicitous"?

WALT. No, not that.

TIM. "Slimy?"

WALT. No, I – . "Slimy?" You think I couldn't recall the word "slimy"?

TIM. Well I don't know, I'm / just trying to –

WALT. I'll find it, it's – . Just let me find it.

(**TIM** *looks at the fireplace.*)

TIM. You starting a fire?

WALT. Oh, I couldn't – . I couldn't get it going.

(**TIM** *goes to the fireplace.*)

TIM. Walt you just stacked the wood, no wonder it's not catching.

WALT. I was distracted.

TIM. You have newspaper?

WALT. *(motioning to the kitchen)* Yeah, you know where it is.

(**TIM** *takes some newspaper out of a drawer in the kitchen, starts to make a fire.*)

WALT. Quite a way to go out, huh? Very last boy I ever have up here, I lose him out in the forest?

TIM. We haven't lost him yet.

WALT. Spending all night out there, I don't – . I don't know.

TIM. There's plenty of streams out there, could find a thing or two to eat if he had to. Someone could survive a while out there.

WALT. I don't know, he was – . He was slight.

(pause)

TIM. You know who I heard from the other day?

WALT. Who?

TIM. That boy, Alan – something?

WALT. Alan?

TIM. Remember, the, uh – . Sixteen, seventeen years ago? He was from Indiana or something, he was the one who loved that Dungeons and Dragons game?

WALT. Oh – right.

TIM. He told me that you stayed up with him until two in the morning one night, letting him teach you how to play it.

WALT. It was so convoluted, I had no idea what he was saying to me.

TIM. He had heard something about you retiring, shutting down. Wanted to get in touch.

(pause)

He told me that he had been sent to three or four groups before that, I guess. All around the country. And he said that you were the only one who would just sit with him and *listen*, that you wouldn't just be spouting off about scripture or sin all the time. That you really just – listened to him. He said that after spending six weeks here, with you, he knew what it must have felt like to have a good father.

(pause)

And he has two boys of his own now, six and ten I think.

WALT. Well, there's one then, but – ...

TIM. What?

WALT. Nothing.

*(***TIM*** lights the fire. He goes to **WALT.**)*

TIM. No, what?

(pause)

WALT. Tim, we both know how many boys have come through here over the years. And we both know how many of them were actually able to –

TIM. It's not like we keep in touch with *all* of them, it's – … You had a positive impact in these boys' lives, we both did, even if they fell back into it later in life we gave them tools / to work on –

WALT. And how many of them fell back into it after getting married, having children? Not to mention the – . God help us, the *suicides* –

TIM. Now *stop*, we don't have complete control over this, sin is a powerful thing, it's – .

(pause)

Walt, what is it that you're getting / at here?

WALT. I just want to be sure that we did *good*, that we didn't *hurt* them, or – .

*(Silence. **TIM** stares at him.)*

TIM. You know how I mentioned to you that I was counseling a boy right now, out of my office? Do you know how old this kid is? Take a guess.

WALT. What?

TIM. Seriously, guess.

WALT. Tim, I don't know / how –

TIM. Twelve. He's twelve years old. He's in the sixth grade, he's in *elementary school*. When you and Abby started doing this, how old were the youngest ones you had up here? Sixteen, *maybe* fifteen?

(pause)

Look, I know what people say about me, they don't understand how I can come up here every summer to work with you. Even within the church, I know people talk, they don't understand why I suddenly became so obsessed with this one issue. I tell them – it's not about this one issue, it's about the culture.

WALT. Tim, I understand, you know / that I –

TIM. No, Walt, actually I'm not sure if you do understand. You've been up here in the mountains for thirty years, you don't know what it's like down there anymore. When Abby and I got married, and she told me about this place – I admit, I didn't totally understand it. But eventually, I looked around and I realized – I'm in the middle of a culture that's shifting by the minute, that's replacing morality with – with *fashion*, that's redefining everything we think about God and – ... When I first started coming up here fifteen years ago, there were four other programs in the state. When this place shuts down, I think I might be the only one left in the *entire Northwest* –

WALT. Tim, I'm not saying / that you –

TIM. And now you're telling me that all the time we've been *hurting* these boys? Walt, that boy isn't out there wandering in the forest because of something that you did here, he is out there because the *culture* has made him lost, made him *disgusting*, made him –

(The phone rings. And rings.)

(Finally WALT goes to the phone, answering it.)

(WALT listens for a minute, then slams the phone down on the receiver.)

(silence)

I'm sorry, I didn't mean to – .

(pause)

Sorry, I didn't mean to climb up on the pulpit just now, but I – . I mean, if you don't have faith in this, then – ...

(TIM trails off, becoming upset. WALT goes to him.)

WALT. We did good work.

TIM. Yes, we did.

WALT. You're still doing good work.

TIM. Yes, I am.

WALT. I just – ...

(pause)

We've spent a lot of time here together. I don't want to lose our friendship.

(pause)

TIM. Well of course not. Why would you – ...?

(pause)

What do you mean?

(**WALT** *looks at him for a moment, then goes back to the dictionary, picks up the magnifying glass, starts searching through it again.*)

WALT. You can go back to bed. If I hear anything I'll wake you.

(**TIM** *watches him.*)

Scene Three

*(Later that morning. **ABBY** is on the telephone. **EUNICE** is watching the Shady Grove DVD, having not slept at all.)*

VOICEOVER ON THE TELEVISION. / – is to provide the highest possible care for our patients who need the assistance of rehabilitative and/or licensed nursing staff. Rehab or skilled care is about more than providing care twenty-four hours a day. It's about being there to listen. Our residents benefit from supportive services and custom healthcare options. Assisted living communities provide or coordinate oversight and services to meet residents' individual needs.

ABBY. Gary, can you – ? Sorry, this dang phone, it's so old, I can barely –

*(**ABBY** bangs the receiver against a wall or counter.)*

Gary? There we go, this is better, keep going.

(pause, listens)

No I'm handling everything, so it's not really – . Well of course he's – .

*(**WALT** enters from outside, goes to **EUNICE**.)*

WALT. Heard anything?

EUNICE. *(still watching the TV)* No.

WALT. You really have to watch that?

EUNICE. I'll keep it low.

ABBY. *(on the phone)* Sure. Yep, I'll be in touch then. Bye.

*(**ABBY** hangs up.)*

ABBY. Well! Some good news finally.

WALT. What?

ABBY. I think I may have found a way to help you pay for this retirement home!

WALT. Abby, for Heaven's sake, I thought you had heard something about Daniel –

VOICEOVER ON THE TELEVISION. / Services are based on the residents' service plans, taking into account unforeseen needs as they arise. Typical services offered in assisted living include those found in housing with services communities, or expanded versions of those services, as well as assistance with daily activities such as bathing, grooming, dressing, and medication administration or management.

ABBY. I had done a little fishing around about the land and whatever, and I've found someone who sounds *very* interested, they want / to take a trip up here –

WALT. Abby, I don't want you making any deals, / I haven't agreed to sell this place –

ABBY. I haven't made a *deal*, this is just talk, I'm just trying to –

WALT. Who are they, anyway?

ABBY. Hm?

WALT. Who is it who wants the –, who's interested in it?

ABBY. Well it's a church!

WALT. Okay?

ABBY. I guess they're interested in starting some sort of camp type thing, / or –

WALT. What church / is it?

ABBY. And they have some time in the next couple weeks to take a trip up here –

WALT. Abby.

VOICEOVER ON THE TELEVISION. Some assisted living communities / have designated areas and programming for individuals who require highly specialized care. This level of assisted living provides services tailored to every individual resident's needs. The care and services that are offered foster skills and interests within an environment that seeks to diminish fear and promote safety. We offer a full continuum of care for seniors and others in the greater Boise and Treasure Valley community. As the only Christian not-for-profit long-term care community in the greater Boise area, we are known for our quality and excellence of service. Founded in 1964, we are also one of the area's oldest and most respected assisted living communities. We have built our business on a reputation for providing consistent care and respect to residents on a wide spectrum of physical and mental health.

ABBY. It's the Life Fellowship people.

WALT. No.

ABBY. I just want you to keep an open mind about this.

EUNICE. Dennis *hates* the Life Fellowship people.

WALT. Well Dennis and I agree on something then. This watered down doctrine, they have no idea what they even believe, they don't / even –

EUNICE. Oh he doesn't care about that, he bought four old vans from them last year and three of them broke down already.

ABBY. Look, Walt, we have our disagreements but you can't argue that a church taking over this place really isn't the / best –

WALT. What kind of "camp" are they talking about, what do you mean?

ABBY. Well I think they want sort of like a retreat, something like that.

WALT. A "retreat"?

ABBY. Oh, Walt, I don't know, they were just talking about something like – some place where the adults could meet / for –

WALT. So they want a place for a bunch of businessmen from Boise to come and get drunk –

ABBY. Well for gosh sake Walt, I thought you'd appreciate me putting in the effort, not like I'm getting paid for this.

(The phone rings.)

WALT. Look it's not that I'm not grateful, I just want to have a say in this.

ABBY. Well of course you have a –

*(**ABBY** answers the phone.)*

VOICEOVER ON THE TELEVISION. / Shady Grove is particularly known for their art therapy program which works with patients suffering from Alzheimer's and related dementias. We offer courses in painting and sculpture, as well as workshops in drama, dance, poetry, and memoir. At Shady Grove, we believe that a healthy mind is an active mind, and that freedom of expression is key to allowing seniors to remain vital, present, and engaged with their surroundings. We strive to allow our seniors to pursue their lifelong hobbies and interests while continually introducing them to new activities. By exercising their minds and bodies on a daily basis, our seniors are made to feel productive and vital. This philosophy has been carefully developed over decades of providing care to seniors.

ABBY. Hello?

*(listens, then to **EUNICE**)*

Eunice.

EUNICE. Who is it?

ABBY. Dennis.

*(**EUNICE** gets up, takes the phone. She takes the receiver back to the couch with her, stretching the cord almost as far as it will go. She sits down, continues to watch the DVD.)*

ABBY. Okay listen Walt, I know this isn't your favorite church or whatever –

EUNICE. *(on the phone)* / Hello.

ABBY. – but they seem pretty interested and that Shady Grove place is by no means cheap, / and we –

WALT. Well maybe I'm not – .

ABBY. What?

EUNICE. / No, they haven't.

WALT. Nothing, this is just – . This is happening too fast.

EUNICE. *(on the phone)* / Yes, well, they're looking. I don't know, he had a coat? I don't know, Dennis. I wasn't here when he left.

ABBY. Wait, what were you going to say?

WALT. I've just been – . I've been thinking about it, and maybe I'm not sure I'm ready to leave yet.

ABBY. *What?*

EUNICE. *(on the phone)* / Well I just didn't want to bother you, you're so important, you hate to be bothered by little things like your son missing in the forest.

WALT. Look I just don't see why I have to act like I'm at death's door or something, I don't see why I –

EUNICE. / Okay.

ABBY. Walt, no one likes growing old, but you – . Tim said you couldn't even figure out how to make a fire last night –

WALT. *I wasn't –* ! That's *not true –*

VOICEOVER ON THE TELEVISION. / Situated on a picturesque plot of three acres as the base of the Boise foothills, Shady Grove's atmosphere is one of tranquility, peace, and reflection. A babbling brook flows just behind Shady Grove's parking lot. A series of gentle, well-lit walking trails surround Shady Grove's perimeter, allowing residents the chance to get their daily exercise while admiring the beauty of God's creation.

EUNICE. *(on the phone)* / Yes, they've sent people for him, they called Search and Rescue. Well, yeah, you could actually come here, that would be something you could do.

ABBY. What if something happens to you up here, what if you fall down again, or –

WALT. *I'm not a cripple for Heaven's sake –*

ABBY. I didn't say that, but you can't really expect Tim and I to drive five hours down here / to –

WALT. Fine then, don't come! I'm an adult, I can handle this by myself!

EUNICE. *(on the phone)* / No, I know, you're important, stay home. I'm not being passive aggressive, I'm just stating a fact, you're so important. You're so, so important.

ABBY. Oh would you stop it with the histrionics?

WALT. I don't know why you two feel the need to come here and treat me like I'm a child or / something –

ABBY. Why we feel the need to – ?! You asked us to come!

VOICEOVER ON THE TELEVISION. / Residents have easy access to a well-maintained 18-hole golf course, as well as tennis and squash courts, all found within five miles of Shady Grove. Daily shuttles provide easy access, and full-time residents can receive special discounted rates on yearly memberships. If you have any questions about these memberships, please call our information line. One of our employees will be happy to assist you.

WALT. *(to* **EUNICE***) Would you please turn off the TV?*

EUNICE. *(to* **WALT***)* I'm good thanks.

(on the phone, rising in intensity)

/ Oh that sounds good, you pray for him. As long as you pray for him I'm sure this'll all work out, that sounds good. So you've done your best here, you've put in so much effort, you've really taxed yourself, so I guess we're done talking.

ABBY. You know Walt, I'm really not appreciating your tone right now, I have to say.

WALT. Well I just don't care, I'm not selling this place, I'm not moving into that stupid retirement home, I'm not just handing over all this to a pack of idiots so they can come up here and drink themselves stupid –

VOICEOVER ON THE TELEVISION. / When residents enter our main complex, they are greeted with a welcoming lobby –

EUNICE. *(on the phone)* / Okay love you bye honey.

> (**EUNICE** *drops the phone on the ground, continues to watch the DVD.*)

ABBY. *(severe)* You could *die* up here Walt, you get worse every month, you / don't –

WALT. *(to* EUNICE*)* TURN OFF THE DAMN TELEVISION, TURN IT OFF.

VOICEOVER ON THE TELEVISION. – as well as a restaurant-style dining hall that always offers residents their choice of entrée, side dish, and –

> (**EUNICE** *turns off the television, looks at* **WALT.** *Silence.*)

WALT. I'm sorry.

> *(Pause.* **WALT** *breathes.)*

EUNICE. Yeah I'll give you two a minute.

> (**EUNICE** *takes her coffee and exits down the hall. Pause.*)

ABBY. I need you to be *reasonable* about this –

WALT. I *do not* get worse every month.

ABBY. Okay.

WALT. And *I know how to build a fire.*

ABBY. *Okay.*

> *(pause)*

Alright I'm not *bickering* with you anymore. Lord, you'd think we were still married.

> *(Silence.)*

WALT. I'm sorry.

ABBY. Hm.

WALT. *I'm sorry.*

> *(pause)*

Do you – ...? I'm starving, are you hungry?

(pause)

ABBY. Yeah, I could eat something.

*(***WALT*** goes into the kitchen, roots through the fridge a bit. ***ABBY*** sits down.)*

WALT. We don't have – . Well, we don't have much of anything actually.

ABBY. Sandwiches?

WALT. We don't have any more bread.

ABBY. Lunch meat?

WALT. Bologna.

ABBY. Ech. Bring it over.

*(***WALT*** takes a package of bologna out of the fridge, brings it to ***ABBY***.)*

WALT. I'm sorry to be so – . It just feels wrong, talking business with all this going on.

ABBY. Look, I know you're not *relishing* this, giving this place up. But I really think you should just sell it while there's someone who's interested. It's just smart.

*(***WALT*** opens up the package of bologna, takes a piece out, starts eating it. ***ABBY*** does the same.)*

WALT. Life Fellowship, of all people.

ABBY. Walt.

*(Pause. ***WALT*** looks at ***ABBY***.)*

WALT. I'm not leaving.

(pause)

ABBY. So you're just gonna stay up here until you have an accident or something. Until you fall down again, but this time you can't reach the phone, and you just lie on the floor / and –

WALT. Yes.

(pause)

Yes.

(The door opens and **TIM** *appears followed by* **JANET**, *more serious than before, holding a plastic bag.)*

TIM. Hi –

WALT. Find anything?

JANET. Well, uh. Yeah, we did.

> (**JANET** *reaches into the bag, pulling out the jacket* **DANIEL** *was wearing before.*)

JANET. Was this – was he wearing something like this when he left?

> (**WALT** *looks.*)

WALT. Yes. Yeah, I think that was it, but let me –

> (*calling down the hall*)

> Eunice!

TIM. Wait, it might not be a good / idea –

WALT. No, just – she'll know best, she remembers what he was wearing when he left –

> (**EUNICE** *appears in the hall, she sees the jacket.*)

EUNICE. Is that – ? Where did you find it?

JANET. You think this is his?

EUNICE. I think so, where did you find it?

JANET. A fire jumper found it, little over ten miles south of here. Close to where the fire's been heading. This is the right color, this is – ?

> (**EUNICE** *takes the jacket.*)

EUNICE. Yeah, it –

> (**EUNICE** *unfolds the jacket. One side is covered with a large blood stain.*)

> (*Silence.*)

JANET. Is this – ? You're sure it's his?

> (**EUNICE** *doesn't answer, continues to look at the jacket.*)

JANET. Okay. I guess we – .

> (*pause*)

> Well, see – this sorta changes things.

Scene Four

(Shortly later. WALT *looks out a window,* ABBY *sits.* TIM *paces.)*

TIM. You know, I just don't – . I don't want us to jump to any conclusions here, we have no idea if he – . I mean, are we even sure it's his jacket?

ABBY. Tim.

TIM. I'm just saying. Even if it's his, we can't be sure that he's – …

(pause, looking down the hall)

What's Janet saying to her in there?

ABBY. They're not plotting against us, you don't / need to –

TIM. I just don't want Janet getting her worked up, get her / thinking that –

WALT. I don't know why we're all just sitting around here, we could be doing something –

ABBY. Like what?

WALT. Well I don't know, we could be driving around ourselves, or –

ABBY. There are plenty of people out there looking for him who are much / more qualified –

TIM. But I mean it hasn't even been twenty-four hours yet, I could head toward where they found the jacket, I could take the car as / far as –

ABBY. Alright, I'm sorry, but do you two really think – …?

(pause)

WALT. What?

(pause)

ABBY. Look, I don't know anything about anything, but if he's lost that much blood, and been out there all night – … I'm not saying we should have a funeral, I'm just saying –

WALT. Saying that we should give up?

(pause)

ABBY. I'm saying we need to be *realistic* about this.

TIM. Sure, but is it really time to stop looking?

ABBY. Of course not, everyone is still out there looking for him, but I'm just saying that we – the three of us should – …

(pause)

Look, I realize how this sounds, but I think we should start thinking about what to do, you know, what Walt should be saying to the media, just in case –

WALT. "The media."

(Short pause.)

ABBY. What?

WALT. "The media," there's a child out there, alone, and you're worried about – . It's all about appearances with you, isn't it? All about what people will think of us, it's never about the boy, it's never about Isaac, it's just about what people will think about *us*, it's / about –

ABBY. What did you just say?

(pause)

WALT. I just mean, you don't need to be constantly concerned with what people will think of us, people will think whatever / they –

ABBY. You said "Isaac."

(pause)

WALT. No, I didn't.

ABBY. Yes you did, you said "Isaac."

TIM. Okay, / okay –

WALT. Well I didn't – . I meant "Daniel," I obviously meant "Daniel," I / just –

ABBY. No you didn't. No, you didn't.

*(Pause. **ABBY** looks away.)*

ABBY. You know, maybe – …

(pause)

I think maybe it'd be a good idea for us to get out of here for a little / while –

TIM. Okay now, you've known each other too long to talk to each / other like –

ABBY. Tim, it's okay, I'm not – . I just think it'd be best for us to get a room in town for the / night.

WALT. Oh for heaven's / sake –

TIM. Now c'mon, let's just take a minute and catch / our breaths –

ABBY. Tim, could you get our bags?

WALT. *(harsh) Abby, would you please not fall to pieces over this?*

(Silence. **ABBY** *stares at him.)*

ABBY. After everything I've done here, everything I've done for you over the years, and now trying to help you *sell* it –

WALT. I never asked you to / sell this place –

ABBY. – and you bringing this kid up here at the last minute without even telling us, letting him wander outside *alone*, leaving us to deal with – …

(pause)

You really think I did all of this for *appearances*, is that what you think?

WALT. *Well you did, didn't you?* You were so *ashamed* at mothering some kid who turned out that way, so concerned that people / thought –

TIM. *Okay guys, we –* …

(silence)

Look, maybe Abby's right, maybe we should get out of here for a while –

ABBY. *(to* **TIM***)* Could you get our bags?

*(***TIM** *looks at her, then at* **WALT.***)*

ABBY. Please.

(Pause. **TIM** *exits down the hall.)*

ABBY. I supported you through all of this, taking over this place, starting this program. You think it was easy for me, going to all those churches, giving those talks about Isaac?

WALT. Oh let's be honest, Abby, you never minded the attention, / you didn't –

ABBY. *I loathed the attention. I loathed it.*

(pause)

I would get up there in front of all those parents and tell them about my son, about the *failure* of my life, my motherhood. For you, starting this place was – helpful, *healing* even, you got to come up here and go on hikes and light campfires and everyone thought you were so *noble* and so *good* –

WALT. You think I've been on some sort of vacation up here?! I've spent my entire *life* trying to save these boys, and now you're ready to give up on this place, just like you gave up on Isaac.

(short pause)

And that was *your* failure, not his. And it was my failure too, I let it happen. But I've dedicated my *life* to making up for that mistake, while you've just been running away from it. That's why you stopped coming up here, that's why you want to shut this place down. That's why our marriage ended, you know that.

(pause)

ABBY. Walter, our marriage ended because you never loved me.

(Silence.)

WALT. That's not true.

ABBY. I don't blame you.

WALT. That's not true.

ABBY. You're not capable of – .

> (**ABBY** *stops herself. Silence.*)

> (**TIM** *re-enters with the suitcases, looks at them.*)

> (*pause*)

ABBY. (*to* **WALT**) I'm going to tell the Life Fellowship people that they can go directly through you. They have your number.

> (*pause*)

Just sell it, Walt. It's over. Allow it to be over.

> (**ABBY** *exits, taking her suitcase.* **TIM** *goes to* **WALT**.)

> (*They look at one another for a brief moment.*)

WALT. I'm sorry, / I don't –

TIM. It's fine, we – . We won't be far. Let's just – ... Let's just let everyone cool down a bit.

WALT. Sure.

> (**TIM** *and* **WALT** *look at one another for a moment.*)

> (*Finally,* **TIM** *extends his arm for a handshake.* **WALT** *looks at him.*)

TIM. We'll see you soon. Okay?

> (**WALT** *looks at him for a moment longer, then shakes his hand.* **TIM** *takes his suitcase and exits,* **WALT** *watches him go.*)

> (*From outside we hear the sound of a car starting up, driving away.*)

> (**JANET** *enters.*)

JANET. Hey, Walt. So like I was just explaining to Eunice, all this means is that we're pulling out all the stops now.

WALT. Okay.

> (**EUNICE** *enters slowly from the hallway.*)

JANET. Sheriff's got more support coming up from Boise, they're gonna start focusing the search around where the jacket was found, if he dropped it there within / the last –

EUNICE. *(to* **JANET***)* Give us a minute. If that's okay?

(pause)

JANET. Okay then. I'll just be, uh – .

*(***JANET*** goes outside.* **WALT** *goes to* **EUNICE***.)*

WALT. Eunice, I can't tell you how sorry I am, but I – . I *promise* we are not giving up, we *will* find / him –

EUNICE. Walt, *please*, you don't have to – …

(pause)

Janet did this thing, she was like – … She was being so *positive* about everything, she – . But – realistically? – he's not coming back, is he?

WALT. We don't – . That's not certain / that he's –

EUNICE. Walt, *did you see his coat?* He has no idea how to survive out there in the woods, when his dad took him camping he could barely take ten steps without falling down or cutting himself, you think after being out there *all night,* and losing that much blood –

WALT. It's been less than twenty-four hours, and we / have no idea –

EUNICE. Are you worried that I'm going to sue you? Because you don't need to worry about that, if that's what / you –

WALT. *No,* I'm not – . There's just no use in jumping to conclusions, assuming that / he's –

EUNICE. Well there is some use *for me*, there's some use for me in thinking that he's *dead*, that he's not going to come back, that he – .

(pause)

Walt – say he comes back. Say he walks through that door, right now. Then what?

WALT. Look, there are – . Obviously he shouldn't continue on with me, but –

EUNICE. Okay, so we shove him into the next program, and the next one, and the next one... Eventually he marries someone he's not in love with, has *kids*? Lives the rest of his life beating himself down?

(pause)

Or – we let him leave, he tries to make a life within it. He turns his back on God, God turns his back on *him,* and he – ...

WALT. *Or,* he works, and eventually finds real, meaningful change –

EUNICE. He lives with a man who can't stand to admit that he's his father. He *hates* himself. If that wasn't enough of a motivation to change, then excuse me but what would you or anyone else have to say that would be?

(pause)

What would be best for him – is if he never came out of that forest. If he curled up under some tree, and felt the sun on his face, and just – . And I say that as a mother who *loves* him. A mother who can't stand the thought of never seeing him again.

(Pause. EUNICE goes to the door, opens it up. She lets JANET inside.)

EUNICE. *(to* JANET*)* You have my cell phone number, right?

JANET. Uh – sure?

EUNICE. You can call if you find anything.

(pause)

JANET. Wait, are you – ? You're leaving?

EUNICE. Yeah.

JANET. Well are you gonna be in town, or – ?

(EUNICE grabs her purse, heads to the door. She stops, turns to WALT.)

EUNICE. He's better off out there. You know that.

(EUNICE exits. JANET watches her go. The sound of a car door opening and shutting, an engine starting up, a car driving off.)

JANET. Well what the hell is she doing?

WALT. I think she's – going home.

(Pause. JANET watches her drive off.)

JANET. Well I know that she's upset, but geez. I mean I was pretty clear with her, we don't know anything for certain. We really don't.

WALT. Sure.

JANET. Was it something I said to her? I just hope I / didn't –

WALT. No, Janet, it's – . You're fine.

(pause)

What do you think?

JANET. About the kid?

(pause)

Well look, you just never know, I mean he could be out there wandering around still, maybe / he's –

WALT. Janet. What do you really think?

(Long pause. JANET thinks.)

JANET. I think – .

(pause, direct)

I'd say at this point we're looking for a body.

(pause)

I'm sorry, Walt.

(WALT sits down. Silence.)

JANET. Listen, Walt. I'm not trying to whatever, psychoanalyze you or whatever, but I don't want you thinking this is somehow your fault. Christ, he's not a five-year-old, it wasn't your fault he wandered off. What, were you supposed to keep him on a leash?

(pause)

You know, when I first moved out here, took this job –
people told me about you. Some religious nut out in
a cabin, brings in all these gay kids, converts them or
whatever. I thought it was bat-shit crazy, to be honest.

WALT. You did?

JANET. Sure. I mean, I got nothing against gays. My cousin
Shelly, she's been living with her partner for decades,
happy as shit. Live and let live, that's what I say. So
when I heard about you, I had this idea that you were
hurting these kids, or – .

(pause)

I don't know about this conversion stuff, but one thing
I do know? You weren't hurting these kids. You weren't
forcing them to do or say anything. You took care of
'em.

(Silence. **JANET** *looks at him.)*

JANET. Right?

*(***WALT** *looks at her.)*

Scene Five

*(The next morning, just before dawn. **WALT**, tired and unkempt, is bending down in front of the fireplace, trying to make a fire.)*

(The Shady Grove DVD plays in the background.)

VOICEOVER ON THE TELEVISION. – a welcoming lobby, as well as a restaurant-style dining hall that always offers residents their choice of entrée, side dish, and dessert. All of Shady Grove's common areas are easily accessible from every apartment.

*(The phone rings, **WALT** goes to it. He listens for a moment, then hangs up the phone with his finger, drops the receiver on the floor.)*

All of our buildings are single-level, making moving easy for any resident, regardless of physical ability.

*(**WALT** pokes at the fire a few times unsuccessfully. He gets up, going to the kitchen, looking for some paper.)*

The dementia care program, "Understand Their Journey," is designed with a clear understanding of memory loss in order to provide the best resident focused care. Our premise is simple: understand residents in their moment, rather than try to force them into our reality.

*(**WALT** continues to search through the kitchen, unable to find any paper. He looks up, sees the dictionary in the room.)*

By using this approach, we validate the resident's worldview and reality and allow them to live their lives in a way that feels familiar. Our caregivers focus on knowing a resident's wants, needs and preferences based on their life story.

*(**WALT** goes to the dictionary, looks at it briefly, then tears several pages out of it. He continues to rip pages*

out, filling his hands. He goes to the fireplace, shoves the
papers inside the fire.)

Understanding the resident's past experiences and
preferences allows us to provide for their needs at every
stage of their memory loss. We honor and validate our
resident's reality, and support them to be purposeful
and successful each day.

(**WALT** *lights the pages, the fire starts immediately. He*
slowly begins to stand up, has a sharp pain in his hip
and nearly falls over. He steadies himself, wincing.)

We also join the journey of families through support,
education, and ongoing communication. We hold
family orientations, supply a resource library, and
offer family support groups. We also issue monthly
publications which we call "Moments," highlighting a
family member's treasured moments in life, and share
those with the greater memory care community.

(**WALT** *heads back to the kitchen, looks for some food.*
He sees the paper bag holding the heirloom tomatoes. He
takes the bag, reaches inside, pulling out the purple one
from before. He looks at it.)

Most importantly, we offer our residents suffering from
dementia a caring, compassionate staff who undergo
specialized dementia care training.

(**WALT** *starts to eat the heirloom tomato.)*

Understanding how dementia affects the brain
helps each caregiver better understand behaviors,
communication barriers, and the overall needs of each
patient.

(The door opens and **DANIEL** *appears. He is dirty,*
gaunt, and shining.)

(The sound of the fire from before is heard, steadily
increasing in volume.)

(He looks at **WALT.** **WALT** *continues to eat the heirloom*
tomato, not noticing **DANIEL.***)*

For residents needing care in speech rehabilitation, Shady Grove offers several services, most of which are typically covered by Medicare Part B.

(WALT senses someone looking at him, turns around, sees DANIEL.)

(WALT drops the tomato. WALT and DANIEL stare at one another, silent.)

(The sound of the fire continues to grow, filling the space.)

Treatment plans include recovery of speech, language and memory skills, non-verbal communication, diet recommendations –

(The sound of the fire drowns out the television, the lights snap to black.)

(The sound continues in the darkness for a few moments before lights rise on:)

Scene Six

(Shortly later, dawn. **DANIEL** *sits on the couch,* **JANET***, just woken up and not in her uniform, is bandaging a wound on his leg. A few mostly eaten heirloom tomatoes sit on the table in front of* **DANIEL***, along with the bologna.)*

*(***WALT*** stands on the other side of the room, looking at* **DANIEL***.)*

JANET. You feeling faint at all, any dizziness?

*(***DANIEL*** shakes his head.)*

Numbness in your hands or feet, anything like that?

*(***DANIEL*** shakes his head again.)*

Walt – could you get him some more water?

*(***WALT*** looks at* **DANIEL***, saying nothing.)*

Walt?

WALT. Oh, uh – . Yeah, I'll – .

*(***WALT*** goes to the kitchen, fills up a glass of water.)*

JANET. You look okay to me, but I'm no doctor, so I think I should take you into town.

*(***WALT*** comes out of the kitchen, bringing the glass of water to* **DANIEL***.)*

(to **WALT***)*

This cut doesn't look too deep, but we really should have someone look at it, just in case he needs stitches –

DANIEL. I have to – . I think I might have – …

(Pause. **DANIEL** *stares at* **WALT***.)*

WALT. Daniel –

DANIEL. I think I might have talked with God.

(Pause. **WALT** *and* **DANIEL** *stare at one another.)*

JANET. O – kay then.

(short pause)

JANET. *(cont.)* I'll be right back, I just wanna radio some people, let them know you're okay.

(JANET heads toward the door. WALT looks at her.)

I'll be right outside. You – you keep him here, yeah?

(to DANIEL)

I'll give your mom a call. She's sure gonna be glad to hear you're okay, yeah?

(JANET exits.)

(pause)

DANIEL. I'm sorry for leaving like that –

WALT. It's okay –

DANIEL. But I think it was meant to happen this way. I've realized something, something so important, and I – …

(Pause. WALT goes to DANIEL.)

DANIEL. When I was out there, when I started wandering – I was thinking about middle school, my friend Josh who lived outside of town on this ranch? I would go over there during the summers, and we'd spend the nights in this airstream outside his house, and I – …

(silence)

I loved him. It wasn't about sex, I just – loved him. And I was simple, so I didn't understand what that meant. So I told him how I felt.

(pause)

He told me to never tell anyone else, and that I shouldn't be around him anymore. He told me he would pray for me, that I could gain freedom from these feelings. I see him at school now, he doesn't look at me anymore.

(Pause. WALT goes to DANIEL.)

WALT. Daniel –

DANIEL. I mean I think back to first grade, and even then – I remember having a crush on a boy in my class. In the *first grade*. It was such a part of me that I didn't even think about it, I just – .

(pause)

I thought I was going to die out there, I was *sure* that I was going to die out there, I was sure that God *meant* for me to die out there, that it would just be easier for everyone. But then I tripped on this rock and cut my leg, really deep – and I got my coat and I bandaged it up, and I thought for sure I was, like – . I thought if I wasn't dead already, I was going to die. And I got up, and I walked over this hill and looked down and there was just *fire*. Everywhere.

WALT. There was a forest fire, a storm south of here with some lightning, it had –

DANIEL. It was like God was showing me – the end. Of everything.

(pause)

Like everything was being wiped out. Everything was being killed, turned to ash. Reduced down to something so simple.

(pause)

I looked down, and my leg was healed. Stopped bleeding. I cut myself so deep, I was pretty sure I was looking at *bone*.

(pause)

It was like you said. It was like a baptism.

(Silence.)

(**WALT** *takes* **DANIEL**'s *glass.*)

WALT. Here, Janet said / you should –

DANIEL. And I realized something when I was out there.

(pause)

DANIEL. *(cont.)* Up until that moment – I thought Josh had abandoned me. I thought he was turning his back on me. But I realized – *I'm* the problem, there's something in *me* that isn't right. And if I work hard enough, I *can* change – right?

*(Pause. **WALT** looks at **DANIEL**.)*

WALT. Daniel.

DANIEL. And I know it's still going to be work, but that work can start here, with you. I know that God has given me these feelings for a reason, like you said, it's about overcoming them.

WALT. Daniel –

DANIEL. And I'm ready to –, you know, I'm ready to spend the *rest of my life* working at it. It's like I finally / get it –

WALT. Daniel –

DANIEL. I finally get what everyone has been saying to me, what my dad has been saying to me, all these pastors, I finally / get –

WALT. What did you say to me?

(pause)

DANIEL. What?

WALT. When you left, right before you left. You were standing in that door, and you said something to me. What did you say to me?

(pause)

DANIEL. I said I felt safe with you. I told you I felt safe with you.

(silence)

*(Then, slowly, **WALT** starts to silently break down. His head falls into his hands.)*

DANIEL. No, it's – . Walt, this is good! This is a really good thing. I feel really – good about the future.

*(**WALT** looks at **DANIEL**.)*

DANIEL. And I'm sorry it had to happen like that, I'm sorry I had to scare you. I didn't mean to do that, I wish I could have –

WALT. No, it's not – . It's not that.

(pause)

I just look at you, and you're so young. I think about myself, when I was your age.r

(pause)

I could have been anything.

(Black.)

End of Play